Isabel
clark

Isabel
clark

OX-CART MAN

By DONALD HALL

Pictures by BARBARA COONEY

The Viking Press, New York

Library of Congress Cataloging in Publication Data
Hall, Donald, Ox-cart man.
Summary: Describes the day-to-day life throughout the
changing seasons of an early 19th-century New England family.
[1. New England—Fiction]   I. Cooney, Barbara.   II.   Title.
PZ7.H14115Ox   [Fic]   79-14466   ISBN 0-670-53328-9

For Paul and Bertha Fenton

D.H.

For Elijah

B.C.

In October he backed his ox into his cart
and he and his family filled it up
with everything they made or grew all year long
that was left over.

He packed a bag of wool
he sheared from the sheep in April.

He packed a shawl his wife wove on a loom
from yarn spun at the spinning wheel
from sheep sheared in April.

He packed five pairs of mittens
his daughter knit
from yarn spun at the spinning wheel
from sheep sheared in April.

He packed candles the family made.

He packed linen made from flax they grew.

He packed shingles he split himself.

He packed birch brooms his son carved
with a borrowed kitchen knife.

He packed potatoes they dug from their garden
—but first he counted out potatoes enough to eat all winter
and potatoes for seed next spring.

He packed a barrel of apples

honey and honeycombs

turnips and cabbages

a wooden box of maple sugar
from the maples they tapped in March

when they boiled and boiled and boiled the sap away.

He packed a bag of goose feathers that his children collected
from the barnyard geese.

When his cart was full, he waved good-bye to his wife,
his daughter, and his son

and he walked at his ox's head ten days

over hills, through valleys, by streams

past farms and villages

until he came to Portsmouth
and Portsmouth Market.

He sold the bag of wool.

He sold the shawl his wife made.

He sold five pairs of mittens.

He sold candles and shingles.

He sold birch brooms.

He sold potatoes.

He sold apples.

He sold honey and honeycombs,
turnips and cabbages.

He sold maple sugar.

He sold a bag of goose feathers.

Then he sold the wooden box he carried the maple sugar in.

Then he sold the barrel he carried the apples in.

Then he sold the bag he carried the potatoes in.

Then he sold his ox cart.

Then he sold his ox, and kissed him good-bye on his nose.

Then he sold his ox's yoke and harness.

With his pockets full of coins, he walked through Portsmouth Market.

He bought an iron kettle to hang over the fire at home,

and for his daughter he bought an embroidery needle
that came from a boat in the harbor
that had sailed all the way from England,

and for his son he bought a Barlow knife,
for carving birch brooms with

and for the whole family he bought two pounds
of wintergreen peppermint candies.

Then he walked home, with the needle and the knife
and the wintergreen peppermint candies tucked into the kettle,

and a stick over his shoulder, stuck through the kettle's handle,
and coins still in his pockets,

past farms and villages,
over hills, through valleys, by streams,

until he came to his farm,
and his son, his daughter, and his wife were waiting for him,

and his daughter took her needle and began stitching,

and his son took his Barlow knife and started whittling,

and they cooked dinner in their new kettle,

and afterward everyone ate a wintergreen peppermint candy,

and that night the ox-cart man sat in front of his fire
stitching new harness
for the young ox in the barn

and he carved a new yoke

and sawed planks for a new cart

and split shingles all winter,

while his wife made flax into linen all winter,

and his daughter embroidered linen all winter,

and his son carved Indian brooms from birch all winter,

and everybody made candles,

and in March they tapped the sugar maple trees
and boiled the sap down,

and in April they sheared the sheep,
spun yarn,
and wove and knitted,

and in May they planted potatoes, turnips, and cabbages,

while apple blossoms bloomed and fell,

while bees woke up, starting to make new honey,

and geese squawked in the barnyard,

dropping feathers as soft as clouds.